His education was supported by the wages of his menial job and the minor profits earned from his mother's bakery. The children grew up experiencing the hardships that their mother had endured to make ends meet. As she grew old, however, his siblings went their separate ways. One day, as he sat braiding his mother's hair, tears welled up in his eyes — most of her hair was gone. Wiping his tears away, she asked, "Juan, what's wrong? This is the first time you've cried in years."

He remained silent. Pressing his face against his mother's palms, he wore a smile to veil his grief. He faltered, "Mum, you're old."

Then came his mother's demise. With her gone, he thought no more and set out on an exploration — one that would teach him about the world.

What followed was a mighty journey on a ship that swayed with the waves of the ocean. Neither the dark nights nor the encounters with death could dampen his spirits.

One day, upon sighting a group of lush green islands, one of the travellers called out to his fellow passengers, "Look, islands! They're beautiful!" He observed the land for a long while through his binoculars and overjoyed by the sight, praised the Lord. Together, they gazed in awe at the newfound islands.

Rodriguez — that was the name of the discoverer. "See, the Lord is with us. Like the goal that legitimises the path, a heavenly spectacle lies before us.", he babbled like a man who had struck gold.

"Juan, what's on your mind? You don't look happy in the slightest." Rodriguez pressed his shoulder. Juan smiled at him like a man who had just been woken up from a dream.

"Oh, I really am glad. I was merely lost in the beauty of the land." As he felt the warmth of Rodriguez's palm, Juan felt energised.

As the men celebrated, the ship was fastened to a tree that jutted out from the shore. The cave-like canopy of the trees and the little brooks and lakes made the island a paradise to the weary passengers.

Juan wandered alone with a heavy bag on his back and a cane that was his constant companion. As he approached the picturesque meadow farther in the jungle, he grew happier. A little satchel on his shoulder contained the scales and instruments that he had carried for his research on the island.

Eventually, the memory of his fellow passengers faded from Juan's mind. But years later, he heard the tale of their excesses. Like cattle in pasture, they feasted and trampled on the island and proved themselves to be the greedy merchants they were as they left with whatever they deemed profitable.

It was only after several days that it occurred to Juan that the island was inhabited. The discovery of trails and footprints validated his suspicions. His first contact with the native population was a middle-aged woman. The bark cloth that she had worn had barely concealed her bosom. Lacking a common tongue, they conversed through friendly gestures.

Days later, she, along with several others of her tribe — oung and old, visited Juan.

His life began anew in a bamboo hut, sheltered and ꞈed by the steady flow of life all around him.

<u>Degogartia's Own Grandpa</u>

The virgin island was the epitome of natural beauty. The tale that each grain on its shores has to narrate is also pure and unblemished. The deep blue oceans that surrounded it merged to flow together past its shores. Those waters that join the continents of the world and the islands too had stories to tell. The ocean, the home of varied aquatic beings witnessed never-ending currents that turned warm and cold. Wild at the coast and calm far away from it was the very nature of the ocean. But when the skies turn dark, it grows rough. Sometimes, even the land seems to sway with the Universe.

In the days of past, men from foreign lands would arrive at its shores to plunder its wealth and beauty. In an age when scientific knowledge had not yet flourished, despite being driven by greed, these voyages were often risky and the voyagers fearless. Braving dangerous trenches and waves and at moments, facing death, they emerged victorious like warriors in battle.

What followed the fulfilment of the journey was feasting and drinking. The travellers were heavily built men of immense appetite who devoured fruit and flesh indiscriminately.

It was the "gun" – the result of man's immaturity that had motivated and equipped him to conquer the beasts of the wild. In a way, these intruders had destroyed the purity of the islands. Each of these lands should have long stories of cruelty to tell.

The picture painted by the travellers at a different island was one that of extinct trees and birds. As they docked to relish the beauty of the island, their hounds were craving for flesh. The birds who were stirred by the bustle at the shore were lured out of the jungle by the grains scattered by the sailors. Little did they realise that they would be delicacies for the sailors. As these colourful flightless birds danced around on their duck-like feet, the hounds, like their masters, were fixated on their juicy flesh.

These gentle beings were given a name – "Dodo", which in the tongue of the seamen, meant 'idiot'. The eating habits of the dodo were peculiar. The island was home to trees that bore hard, red fruits which beneath the shell, were sweet. The birds, attracted by its vibrance, would flock around to eat them. The hard fruits, which softened in the guts of the dodos, sprouted into new saplings upon expulsion. Thus, the death of the birds reduced the trees to a memory. Like the old idiom "two birds for one stone", the birds and the trees vanished together.

The story of the island remained vivid in old Juan's memory. He had arrived there as a young man. He alone knew the truth. In his prime, he had travelled across the globe on a ship, a voyage that spanned several months. A journey through vast blue oceans...

The journey was an unexpected one, disrupting his academic aspirations. An industrious young man, he was silent about his ambitions; his plans were his own. In his land where relationships were shallow, break-ups and unions were commonplace. His family was a father whose face he hardly remembers, a mother, and five younger siblings. His father was never a topic in Juan's conversations with his mother. He had left when their marriage turned sour – not different from what had happened in most families.

The tribes led by the woman paid frequent visits to his little shack, often bringing with them cooked yam, honey and grilled fish. They spent time with Juan, watching him eat with great curiosity.

When alone, Juan was immersed in his thoughts. He resolved to transform himself: to dress like them, to speak their tongue, to be one among them. As time elapsed, his hair grew longer and his nails began collecting dirt under them. Wearing battered clothes and sandals, he submitted himself to the ways of the tribe.

Rising early at dawn, Juan would have some tea before setting out to the stream to fish, equipped with a fishing rod, some bait and a creel for the day's catch. Never was he irked by a poor catch – all he wished for was a day's meal... from the freshly baked bread at his mother's bakery to the boiled yams, cooked fish and the strong, warm drink of the island.

His lunch was the generosity of the tribe: each day, someone brought him his share. Whoever brought him the meal was rewarded with the day's catch from which he would spare one for himself.

Following an afternoon nap, he would head out to the shore that teemed with the purity of Nature. The contemplative cranes, with their broad wings and slender legs planted in the white sand, awaiting the little fish that were washed ashore by lashing waves, was a sight to behold. Their cries were indeed clamorous but gazing at them was a feast to the eyes. The waves that fed the cranes raced back into the ocean faster than they came.

The beach was indeed picturesque, but his inquisitive mind led Juan to a tiny colony of algae that grew by the shore. He began studying those round, thick organisms; perhaps they belonged to the genus about which had learned as a graduate student.

The words of Prof. Dean, the foremost microbiologist of those days, echoed in Juan's mind. Perhaps these velvety algae that swayed with the rhythm of the ocean were the exact ones that he had described in his lectures.

During one of his lectures, Prof. Dean, as was customary, talked at length about the medicinal properties of such algae. His eyes sparkled with confidence as he spoke about its potential to cure the most lethal diseases that plagued mankind. Pondering about the professor's ideas, Juan made an important decision.

These aquatic plants that grew in rock crevices exhibited great affinity towards saline water. They required the saltwater of the sea for their survival.

Stepping down, he plucked the youngest bud and returned to his shack with the bud religiously sheltered in his palm.

On a paper pinned to an uneven writing board, he began sketching it; colouring it once he was done. The more he examined the bud, the fonder he grew.

With the bud deposited in a water-filled pot, Juan stayed up, buried in his thoughts. Late at night, with his eyes growing heavier, he fell into a sound sleep as evidenced by his rather loud snore.

Juan woke up to the morning sun filtering into his room. What greeted him was the sight of the tribal woman at his door, beaming at him with a cup of warm tea.

Surprised by her, Juan leapt out of his bed and looked on with a guilty man's face. He was bothered by his slackness and the inconvenience it had caused for others.

Handing him the cup, she stepped out of his hut. After observing the algal specimen that he had collected the previous day, he returned it to its colony at the shore.

The ocean is a mighty vault that holds deep secrets. It was in these very waters that life first took form. Anyone who contemplates on the mysteries of the ocean easily forgets the troubles of the world.

As a boy, Juan had enjoyed listening to his mother's stories. She would start narrating whenever the two of them were by themselves. Once, she spoke of a man at a beach who stood gazing at the undulating ocean and the beautiful skies that arched over it. Noticing a blade of grass dancing with the waves, he asked the ocean, "Dear ocean, why torment this little grass?"

The ocean replied, "This little grass today will be two tomorrow, three the next day and multiply until I am defaced. I risk losing my very name." The ocean that adored purity could not tolerate the grass that marred its appearance.

Juan watched the algae that was continuously washed ashore by the relentless waves. He recalled the import of his mother's story which, he realised, offered him insight into reality.

The young man who spent his mornings with a fishing rod and a creel was a favourite among the islanders. The tribe – children and adults alike, grew fond of him.

After breakfast, Juan was busy writing and sketching anything that caught his fancy. The natives were delighted to see the painting of the middle-aged woman.

The chief remarked, "Marvellous, I see her very self in it!" He embraced Juan, who felt immensely proud of the chief's high opinion of his work.

His studies of the algae were always undertaken behind closed doors; he was keen on maintaining secrecy. During his experiments, he observed the tiniest movements in the solutions with undivided attention and jotted down his conclusions on a paper pad.

Though an honest and loving man who was equally industrious, he was often forgetful, which explained his meticulous records.

Twenty-five years have passed since his arrival. The pocket watch that kept his time also remained a secret, unknown to the natives.

Despite having never seen a timepiece, they would tell the exact time by simple observations of shadows and the sun's incline.

One evening, as he sat with his feet deep in the cool sand of the island, he caught sight of an approaching vessel. His heart raced at the thought of the island being ransacked by reckless savages. As the vessel inched towards the shore, blood boiled in his veins. He cursed them in rage.

As the sun descended into the ocean, its rays mellowed. Like the canvas of a skilled artist, the horizon acquired new hues. Nature, in its heavenly beauty, glorified the Creator.

After a while, Juan focussed on the boat. Some men who had disembarked were busy fastening their transport to the tree that jutted out to the sea using plastic ropes.

He hurried to a nearby tree. Hiding behind its thick trunk, he observed them with a beating heart. He was surrounded by a thicket interspersed with little trees that swayed with the strong wind.

Juan, who was hidden from their view, watched on as they celebrated their arrival. Their jubilance conveyed a sense of great accomplishment.

Among the eight who arrived, Juan noticed a woman in her early years of youth.

The elation grew as they drank beer; some kissed the sand whereas others prayed on their knees.

Eventually, the skies darkened into a moonless night. The passengers were now returning to their vessel on a makeshift bridge. His mind began to wander but every thought of the woman deeply disturbed him. With the night growing around him, he grew conscious of the roaming beasts. With his creel on his shoulder, he headed back.

As he sat in his shack, Juan's mind was occupied by the woman on the ship. Their intention troubled his soul: were they here for the riches or for the knowledge?

Next morning, Juan headed to the stream as usual. Sitting on top of a flat rock on its banks, he threw his baited hook into the calm waters. Adept in his craft, he waited for his big catch, ignoring the little ones that pecked at his bait.

A sudden tug startled Juan. As the bait was drawn deeper, he got up and with his left foot firmly planted, pulled with all his might. The force was so great that he lost his footing and was about to fall when he felt a pair of hands behind him.

"Keep pulling", said the voice as Juan kept at it, paying no attention to the speaker. Gradually, he dragged ashore a large fish – one far larger than any he had ever caught. As the fish gasped for breath, he witnessed the panic of death in its eyes. He broke into tears.

As he grew aware of his surroundings, grief and shame overcame Juan. He turned around to discover his saviour and was surprised to find the young beauty staring back into his eyes.

"If it weren't for me, you'd have fallen off", she said, but paying no attention to her words, Juan gazed into her eyes.

She was slim and fair, with golden hair that adorned her head. Below her lips was a tiny black mole. "Surely, she has to be German.", thought Juan.

He grew uncomfortable. His shabby clothes stunk, his unkempt hair was dry and grimy, and his face was unshaven. "What would she think, filthy old man? A savage fisherman?", his thoughts raced.

With the huge fish on his shoulder, Juan was about to leave when she protested, "You didn't thank me."

"I'm sorry, please forgive me. I'm old now. My ears and memory have grown weak. Please, forgive me."

As they began to walk, he asked her about her whereabouts.

He saw the answers to all his questions in her beautiful eyes. Her dimples reminded him of his young mother. "Didn't she look the same when I was only a child?", he wondered, but chose not to compare her with the memory of his mother. "I am Andrea, call me Ann. I'm here to experience the beauty of the island and to learn about its people, wildlife, and vegetation. But I'm afraid I do not have the answer to where I am headed. Please forgive me."

He was impressed by her. Apart from being pretty, she was also intelligent. She spent the night in his hut as they had grilled fish for supper. As the day broke, she prepared to leave when Juan asked, "Ann, do you know your way back? Wouldn't your friends have been looking for you last night?"

She smiled as she operated a little device. "Look at this", she said.

He stared in awe at the glowing screen. The beach, her boat, and the travellers, all at her fingertips! He was amazed by the growth of technology.

She talked to them. She said, "I lost my way last night and had to stay in a hut. I'm on my way back now. Uncle François, please forgive me. I couldn't find my way in the dark."

"I'm leaving. Perhaps, Uncle François may come looking for me. But I don't want to trouble him. I'll be back again.", she said.

He noted the path she followed. "She's no ordinary woman; they're not mere tourists, they're here to conquer.", he realised.

Fear gripped him as questions grew in his mind. Unable to find answers, he was overwhelmed.

Later in the day, Juan dismantled his shack and hauled the remnants to a distant location. He knew that she would be back and had to evade her eyes.

As promised, Andrea came looking for him the next day and was surprised by the vanished hut. She searched the entire area but could find no traces of Juan. Not giving up, she walked through the forest looking for him.

She found him angling on the banks of the stream. Overjoyed, she ran up to the old man, hugging and kissing him. Her lips soothed his face and revitalised his solitary heart.

"What should I call you?" Juan laughed like the clamorous stream. "Call me whatever you want.", he replied.

"Oh please, what's your name? Or, perhaps you could suggest one."

"In that case, call me the old man of Degogartia."

"I can't call you that! Considering you an old man makes me sad."

"Isn't that why I gave you the freedom to call me whatever you want? I have no regrets."

"Grandpa Uncle Ho… do you like it?", she smiled as her pretty dimples twinkled. "No, the name ought to be shorter - Ho, Uncle Ho, that's much better."

She pulled him closer and kissed him.

Their hears grew closer but they refrained from discussing their past lives. Being the smart scientist that he was, Juan had observed carefully and studied her.

She is German – a descendant of a strong, sharp and beautiful population.

But he had resolved to ask her about everything. The German blood has always prioritised research and expedition.

They were never keen on fulfilling the base desires of mankind; science and philosophy were their chief pursuits. It wasn't dominance but recognition that they sought. The German civilisation that had perished in the great war was one of fire and blade. However, that wasn't the definitive end of the German culture.

It was an evil man's oppression of innocent lives. But, such a misuse of power never ensures lasting victory.

Juan had realised this in his conversations with and observations of her.

One morning, after breakfast, Juan asked her, "Ann, you haven't answered my questions. We've known each other for a while now. Yet, I still seek answers... Tell me, who are you?"

This confrontation must have surprised her. She replied, "Never have I concealed anything. My name is Andrea Chrysostom. I am the eldest child of my parents, Chrysostom and Linda. I have two siblings: a brother and a sister.

We were a working-class family: my father was a welder at an automotive workshop, and my mother had a rare disease. Whatever father had earned was spent on her treatment. In their eyes, the three of us were the only wealth of the family.

Father was very keen on educating the three of us. My brother, after basic education, learned to weld, and soon, started working. His income brought hope and life to the family.

One day father told me, 'Ann, my dear, you must grow up to become an eminent scientist: a renowned and respected one.'

I was taken aback by his words. Nicholas, my brother, had to start working really young to make ends meet. The very thought of his plight paralysed me. Nevertheless, I gave father my word: a decision of which I remain proud.

I had decided to pursue physics. Aspiring to make beneficial contributions towards humanity, I wished to engage in research after my post-graduation.

I dedicated myself to my education. Applied physics – that was my choice of study. Initially, it was a roaring blue sea that spread in all directions. However, once I had dived in, it was a world of wonder. After post-graduation, I joined a prestigious university in Germany for higher education. The physics department was immense, like the vast ocean and the blue sky.

Being the youngest among the research students, I had received a special consideration from the head of the department, Dr Gregory Groom. The student-interview! I still remember that.

Dr Groom was the chairman of the board. The five others were all middle-aged scientists. As I waited, I prayed to the Lord, to my mother who had nursed me, to my exhausted father and to my siblings. Without them by my side, what could I ever hope to achieve?

As he inspected my certificates, Dr Groom's grave expression turned into a gentle smile. "Intelligent girl", he remarked, handing over the certificates to the other members for their scrutiny and assent.

After a brief, private conversation, the chairman said, 'Okay, Andrea' and we shook hands. When I arrived home, I was surprised to find mother, who had been bedridden all her life, sitting on the edge of her bed.

'Mother, we've won! The chairman seems to have accepted me', I told her. As I held my sister close to me, she told me, with twinkling eyes, 'Mother didn't just sit up straight, she took a cup of tea too.' As I embraced mother, she told me, 'Your father and Nicholas would be delighted to hear this.' Flames of hope had begun to light up her mind.

The thesis that I had managed to submit during my research period was approved by the university. Alongside, Dr Groom commented, 'Go ahead.'

Days after days were spent in books and serious contemplation as I roamed libraries. I read everything I could manage to get my hands upon. Yet, I couldn't grow satisfied. In every page that I had read, I saw the haggard face of my father.

'Ann, you should become a great scientist, an asset to the country and the whole of humanity. You should be an angel to those grappling with deadly diseases', his words echoed in my mind."

Tears welled up in her eyes as she spoke.

"Don't be upset, Ann. Be strong; realise your father's dream. I offer you my help." He stood up and wiped her tears. "May these tears turn out to be joyous."

She resumed her story. "When Uncle François decided to go on an expedition with his team, I expressed my desire to join and he permitted."

"Ann, think about it. It will be a demanding journey. You will have nothing but the hope in your heart to rely upon. You'll have to sacrifice a lot", Juan warned her. "I am willing to suffer, Uncle, and with you beside me, I grow stronger", she replied.

"Once the ship was ready, I bade farewell to my family. Holding mother close, I kissed her face, and embraced my siblings.

Father was sitting next to her. His strong arms were growing weaker every day. With great sorrow buried in my heart, I departed.

The bag was firmly secured to my back.

As I boarded the ship, Uncle François reminded me of his instructions for the voyage.

We travelled for days on end. We docked every time we saw land. Bread and wine kept hunger and thirst at bay.

As the ship approached the islands, I grew happy. The beautiful sight from the deck made me all the more eager to set my foot on its shores. We danced in joy.

As the ship was guided towards the island by the wind in her sails, Uncle François fastened her to the trunk of a tree that jutted out to the sea. Some kissed the fresh sand in their palms; others kneeled down in prayer.

I hope that my answer is satisfactory. There is nothing left that is unknown to you", she said, looking at me earnestly. "You're right. Your account is comprehensive and you, you are impressive. What describes our relationship? Friendship? Affection? Love?

Silence is not an effective guard against your onslaught. So, I'll tell you a little about myself too. I had arrived here as a young man with several others. Eventually, when our time here came to a close, I chose to not to follow suit. I chose not to go down the same old path.

My solitary life here helped me imbibe the very spirit of the island. The island had become my home.

But I am not guilty of corrupting its soul. Never have I hurt the plants and beasts who call this land their own. My hands are clean.

As time passed, my life was transformed. I became one among the people of this land. Nothing ever happens without my knowledge. They too call me 'Uncle Ho'.

I vanquished ignorance from their minds. It was a curse of the generations that preceded us. Though reluctant initially, they learned as much as their intellect permitted them. Today, I am adored as their saviour. Not just of the people, but of the entire land." Astonished by his story, she remarked, "You are an extraordinary man."

He explained to her why he was no different from the average man. "We share a common aim but that being said, our days together need not last forever. The two of us led different lives until now and it is bound to remain so."

His words unsettled Ann. "Did he not say that we are merely travellers who met at an inn?"

But he concealed his true intent from her. He felt that the time hadn't come.

One day, as he was angling by the seashore, Ann, pointing at an algal colony, asked him, "Are they therapeutic?"

He listened to her with keen ears. Her words reflected her dedication, curiosity, and ingenuity. "We can try but, without the necessary apparatus, there is not much hope", he replied.

She replied readily, "Don't worry; my shoulder bag holds a miniature laboratory."

The next day, they set up a makeshift laboratory near his bed.

He encouraged and assisted in her efforts. After long hours spent studying chemical reactions, she settled beside him, wiping the beads of sweat on her forehead.

"We are onto something", she commented. "Carry on, my dear", he lauded her efforts. The results of her experiments that spanned several months were duly recorded.

"I think we're approaching the final stage. The progress is assuring. One day, we'll get there", she opined.

The passengers asked Uncle François about Ann's daytime excursions into the forest. "She is a brave girl. No reason to be concerned", he assured them. Yet, he too couldn't help wondering about her motives.

But Ann had never bothered to explain. "A quest for truth, that is all", she'd say.

She clipped her papers and read it out to Uncle Ho. The footnote of each page summarised her findings.

As Ann turned each page, she observed his face impatiently for signs of approval. But she was never disappointed. Though her technique was flawless, her lack of experience and wisdom was apparent. However, he was careful not to dishearten her. He preferred to be seen as an uncivilised islander. A complete revelation, he judged, was not appropriate at the moment. One day, she left earlier than usual. Her company was not likely to stay at the island for much longer.

"I must hustle", she used to say. With the final preparations for the journey complete, she returned to Uncle Ho. Her pleasant expression had faded.

Seeing her gloomy face, he asked, "What happened, Ann? You look worried. Is something troubling you?"

"Oh, nothing much. I just cannot imagine parting with you", she answered. "Don't be so silly, Ann. You are young. There's a long road ahead but you are very much capable of going the distance. Why then should you not leave?", asked Uncle Ho.

As she laid on his chest, Ho listened to her heart wail. Her body was weeping.

"Ann, our lives are spent pursuing perfection. But keep this in mind: there exists an omnipotent force that governs the Universe: a force that is the source of all that is perfect. Every one of us moves forward in life conforming to that power", he said.

Ho's wisdom ignited her mind. She felt that he kept secrets from her. "Perhaps, he could be a magician or a genius in disguise", she thought as she laid on his chest.

She grew aware of the reality that the ship would leave the next day. Everything had been arranged. In a matter of hours, she would have to bid adieu to this island, and to Uncle Ho.

"But how? It feels as if a part of me is being severed. This is unbearable", she lamented. Her heart skipped a beat.

"But the departure is inevitable. My family, who eagerly await my return, I wonder how they're doing. It's been long since I left home. Is mother better now? I hope I could see her walking again. Father must be tired from working for so long. I wonder if they're able to make ends meet with the little that they earn.

Nicholas – his dreams were plucked before they bloomed;

he had to start working at a tender age to help father bear the family burden. My little sister, she'd have grown up by now. I wonder if she attends school or is at home taking care of mother. These questions… I ought to find answers to them.

But these breath-taking islands and more than that, Uncle Ho – they captivate my heart. The innocence of the islanders and the blue sea that surrounds them with its lively, giant waves are priceless. The ocean lays calm like a gentle mother, nurturing the life within. Isn't she the cradle of life?", she thought.

Ho interrupted her, "Ann, what are you thinking about?" He packed her instruments and research papers. Stroking her gently, he said, "Your dreams will bear fruit. The mysteries of this island and my blessings shall be with your forever."

Handing her a heavy stack of papers that had yellowed with age, he said, "This is my gift to you. These papers bear my life's work. I hope they prove to be an asset in your life ahead. Study them with the greatest attention."

In the last page, Ho had written as follows:
"Dear Ann,

When I first set foot on the shores of this island, I too was a young man with noble intentions. I was here on a quest to discover a medicine that could spell the end of all diseases that plagued humanity. Before I started a new life here studying the algae that thrive on the shores for its medicinal properties, I had already completed my post gradual degree. Forty years have passed. My greying hair reminded me that I was not young anymore. Senility had set in but it wasn't mighty enough to interrupt my work.

As you go through these papers, you will find the truth that you seek so vigorously. March onward. Thanking you,

With love,

Uncle Ho"

With the papers and her equipment in her hands, she said goodbye to Uncle Ho. He kissed her forehead and with his hands on her head, blessed her.

On her way back, Ann turned back very often but Uncle Ho never paid attention. With the burden of desires now vanished, his mind grew lighter. He felt liberated.

As the evening grew darker, the ship that had docked at the shore grew livelier. The imminent journey had enthused the people on board. They were eager to leave the island for their homeland.

Juan had a rough night. Skipping supper, he suppressed his hunger and thirst with cold water. He pulled a thick blanket over himself to fight the cold night of the winter, but his eyes remained open.

Tonight, he is free. His shoulders no longer bore the burden. He experienced the bliss of a free man. Unable to sleep, he tossed and turned in his bed. The only rest he could get was a shallow sleep. Something was haunting his mind. His night was no longer calm; unending nightmares tormented him.

The morning rays caressed the dew on the trees as they found their way into Juan's hut. Juan washed his kettle and cup and made himself warm cup of black tea. As the tea washed down his throat, he felt relieved.

Delighted by the Nature that refreshed him every morning, he praised the Creator. He wondered about the elaborate world that the Lord had designed for his creations. He brought life into the world and made it diverse. And once the earth was replete with life, he retreated and remained elusive like a thief.

Despite the Lord having blessed man with a superior intellect, his efforts have been to bring ruin to his fellow beings. Even when he boasts of being the epitome of creation, his follies are countless. As science advanced and brains grew sharper, geniuses were born. It would be closer to the truth to say that these geniuses were brought to life, not born. What one witnesses here is the victory of the Lord's will.

Though it is generally agreed upon that the modern man is the result of millions of years of evolution, nothing is certain. Man may still evolve and a return to his primitive state would hardly be a surprise – a reverse process of sorts.

When difficult ideas tormented his mind, Juan resorted to rational thought. He decided against wearing his shabby outfit when sending off Ann. He dressed up, wore his hunting boots, and took his cane with him. On a second thought, he grabbed his fishing rod and bait.

He knew that the fish driven away from the shore by the ship would return soon after its departure. A grand supper had been ensured.

Juan oiled his flock of hair with his hands. With his fingers, he smoothened his unkempt beard and made preparations for his trip to the beach.

Andrea too, experienced a similar night. Her fellow passengers had fallen into deep slumber after a grand feast.

With great care, she opened her gift lest she should damage the old papers.

The very first pages carried her into a world of wonders. She assimilated the message delivered by Uncle Ho's shapely German letters in the gentle glow of a candle.

"So, he too is a son of Germany. A solitary man sitting on a pile of secrets – that's who he is", she thought. She realized that he was an academician with an exceptional career – an inexhaustible source of knowledge. Each page of the manuscript conveyed to her the intellectual prowess of Uncle Ho. He had gifted her with far more than what she had wished for – she had been entrusted with the end result of a lifetime of intellectual effort.

"I cannot go on anymore. My legs have grown weak. I find myself prone to collapse to the ground at any moment."

Uncle Ho's words filled her with astonishment. She spoke out loud, as if addressed to herself, "Uncle, you are undefeatable. No force of nature, let alone senility can weaken your legs or constrain those thoughts. I shall stand beside you, to strengthen and support you." She read Uncle Ho's words with eyes that were burdened by sleep. He had saved what he wished to tell her and when the time had finally come, he spoke to her through those pages.

Andrea wrapped the papers carefully. They were alive with the words of Uncle Ho. She fell asleep on the bundle – it was late at night and dawn was not very distant. She felt belittled by the intellectual behemoth who had spent his life emancipating the human race. Wonder and astonishment pushed her deeper into sleep.

She was woken up by a pat on her shoulder. Half asleep, she was blabbering nonsense.

"What's the matter, Ann? Couldn't sleep at night?", asked Uncle François.

"I'm alright, Uncle; couldn't sleep. That's all", replied Ann.

"Ok then."

The passengers had woken up and changed into travel attire. Andrea changed too. She noticed that large crates had been stacked at the stern of the ship.

She asked Uncle François, "What do these crates contain?"

"These are invaluable treasures, my dear – the products of the island." Since then, she never spoke to that money-minded man. The ship set sail before noon. Juan looked on in despair as it began to move. He felt paralyzed; drained of his energies.

As the ship turned into a straight line, its side grew visible.

He vaguely saw two men dragging someone to the stern. One of them was thrashing the captive with a long rod.

Juan's heart raced. He feared everything would crumble. He shouted out with all his might, "Ann, don't leave!"

The sight grew more obscure as he called out again,

"Ann, my dear Ann, don't leave me alone."

Before he finished his words, he felt something large being thrown overboard. It splashed with a great sound. The waters whirled and turned turbulent.

The ship moved faster with the wind. The waves lashed at the shore. Ann was swimming towards the shore.

In a moment's time, Juan reached the sandy shores from the rock upon which he had been standing. By then, she had stood up after swimming up to the shore.

He took her in his arms and laid her down. She was exhausted. With her head on his lap, he gently caressed her. Tears welled up in his eyes as he looked at her. He rubbed his hands to provide warmth to her cold cheeks. She opened her eyes.

Juan's eyes found the papers that he had gifted drifting away in the ocean. The sight brought smile to his lips.

The summer heat was amplified by the hot sun. The sunrays helped her warm up as she tried to bring words to her mouth. With the peace of a rebirth, she embraced him.

"Actually, who are you? My uncle, or my guide, or more than that, my savior?", her heart beat faster as she asked. As he brought her close to his chest, it seemed that the waves were returning his papers to the shore. She cried, "Everything is lost! It is your love that's being carried away by the surging sea."

"Leave it, forget it. You've cried too much, Ann. It's about time you stopped", he consoled her.

As they walked towards his hut, the cooling sands of the

beach stuck to their feet. There was little food for supper – four pieces of bread and some warm beverage.

"Uncle, you could've left this to me", she protested.

"Okay, have food now. You're exhausted. Go to bed after supper", he replied.

The night blessed them with sound sleep. Ann, who woke up at dawn, found Juan pacing up and down. "Uncle, didn't you sleep?", she asked.

"Yes, I did. In fact, I haven't slept so well in years. Ann, I have made some decisions. We must leave immediately."

"But why, Uncle?", she asked anxiously.

"We must. I shall tell you why later. Prepare for the journey now."

At noon, their ship home anchored at the shore. The ship was far advanced. The sight of the ship equipped with the latest technology swaying with the waves impressed Ann.

"Luigi, all set? Let's start!" The two of them watched the island as it slowly faded from their sight. Juan suppressed his grief as he witnessed the beautiful island for the last time. Ann was lamenting the loss of the precious papers.

"Ann, why shed tears? What is lost remains lost. There is no point in crying over it. Leave it."

"Uncle, you speak of it with little regard. How can I forget the priceless gift that you had presented me with?"

Three days passed. The ship arrived at the shores of their homeland. She danced in joy, enjoying the beauty of home with eager eyes.

Ann followed Uncle Ho off the ship. Among the crowd awaiting them, she recognized the face of Professor Groom. He had changed: his grey hair and deep- set eyes revealed his advanced age.

She was surprised when Uncle Ho embraced Professor Groom. She wondered if he was still keeping secrets from her.

"Professor Groom, here stands your brilliant young student, Ann Nicolai", Uncle Juan introduced her. The words of praise in the presence of Professor Groom unsettled Andrea. She remained silent as tears welled up in her eyes. Whether out of joy or sorrow, tears washed down her cheeks. Wiping her tears away, Professor Groom consoled her and with paternal affection, embraced her. From a pocket in his long coat, he produced a scroll which he presented to Ann. Growing nervous, she stuttered, "Sir... Uncle... I don't understand. Is this a dream?"

Dr Juan Ho's research paper had been approved by the university. It was the certificate of recognition that Professor Groom had handed her.

She pressed her against the feet of her uncle – the old man of Degogartia, a renowned scientist, her god on earth. With her hands round his feet, she pressed her lips as her tears drenched them.

"Uncle, you are a god to me", she cried out loud.

"No, Ann. You're wrong", Professor Gregory interrupted. "He is a well-known scientist – the saviour of the whole of humanity – Professor Dr Juan Ho. He is a great man who protected you, guided you and made his discoveries yours. He is never a god; he's a God-sent man. Dr Ho had finished his work long before you had started yours. He kept it a secret to help you in your work. This discovery belongs to you, my dear.

Dr Juan's findings can rescue humanity from the grasp of all deadly diseases, valuable findings! What awaits you is a fantastic world where all tears are of joy", he said.

As she received the certificate from the Vice Chancellor, she was overcome with emotion.

The world celebrated Juan. Juan broke his silence, "I dedicate this joy to the whole of humanity and above all, to my ultimate guide, the Almighty."

Professor Groom held nothing back. "Your uncle is the shining star of our institution. His performance during his years as a student remains unparalleled. His post-gradual answer booklet is on display at the university. Perhaps you might have noticed. My dear friend here is a rank holder, a gold medallist, a professor, a researcher and a holder of four doctoral degrees. The list is endless. But his lifestyle is mysterious and astonishing.

One day, he left the country with all his assets. I looked for him in vain. To be exact, he evaded me.

After several years, I received a handwritten letter from Juan. I read it with wonder and joy but the mystery didn't end there.

'Dear Gregory, I am alive. Please forgive me for not having written sooner. But I shall return one day and then, we'll meet.'

That's Juan. He hesitates to reveal even the most essential matters.

He would write to me very rarely. But not on one letter could I find his address. 'I am engaged in a deep meditation. The research is going on. I am hopeful. We shall meet soon', he wrote. But never did he mention you, Ann.

Perhaps there is no one else in this world like him. Anyway, are you happy now?"

"Sure sir", replied Ann as she looked at Juan like witnessing a magical being. The long hair and unkempt beard gave him an uncivilised look. His nails were uncut, and his feet were bare. His teeth had turned yellow. There was little left to differentiate him from the natives of the island.

"Juan, let us sit down for a while", invited Professor Groom. As the conversation grew deeper, Juan reminded, "The theories that we develop today in the name of research had long before been discovered by the great sages of the past. Centuries ago, they relied upon their insight to do what we, even with the aid of modern technology, struggle to achieve. The science of Yoga and the natural sciences are parallel paths leading to the same destination – the redemption of mankind.

But we are missing an important aspect. A researcher dissects a flower in order to study it. He robs it of its beauty and life.

He may claim that it is a necessary sacrifice. However, at the same time, a yogi reveals the unknown not by destruction but through the unison of his body and mind. The yogi and the scientist share a common objective, but their methods differ greatly." He coughed ceaselessly. "Isn't that all there is, my dear Gregory?"

As he stepped forward, Juan said, "I share this joy with each one of you, with the whole of mankind, and with my dear Ann." Expressing his gratitude for the nation's respect, he moved forward slowly. Gradually, he picked up pace.

He grew emotional, not paying attention to the people around him. Realising that he had fulfilled his life, he set his mind free.

"Dear Ann, everything was meant for you... my granddaughter... Your uncle is leaving... do not seek me... I am leaving..."